The Wizard's Promise

The Wizard's Promise

by Suzanna Marshak

Illustrated by Ted Rand

SIMON & SCHUSTER BOOKS FOR YOUNG READERS
Published by Simon & Schuster
New York   London   Toronto   Sydney   Tokyo   Singapore

Simon & Schuster Books for Young Readers

1230 Avenue of the Americas, New York, New York 10020

Text copyright © 1994 by Suzanna Marshak.

Illustrations copyright © 1994 by Ted Rand. All rights reserved

including the right of reproduction in whole or in part in any form.

SIMON & SCHUSTER BOOKS FOR YOUNG READERS is a trademark

of Simon & Schuster. Designed by Vicki Kalajian and Paul Zakris.

The text for this book is set in 18-point Matrix.

The illustrations were done in watercolor.

Manufactured in the United States of America.

10 9 8 7 6 5 4 3 2 1

Library of Congress Cataloging-in-Publication Data

Marshak, Suzanna.

    The wizard's promise / by Suzanna Marshak : illustrated by Ted Rand

      p. cm.

    Summary: When a witch puts an evil spell on a tree already blessed

by a wizard's promise, the fate of a king's castle hangs in the balance.

    [1. Wizards—Fiction. 2. Witches—Fiction. 3. Trees—Fiction.]

I. Rand, Ted, ill. II. Title.

PZ7.M3537Wi 1994 [E]—dc20   92-36507 CIP AC

ISBN: 0-671-78431-5

For my daughter, Elizabeth

—S.M.

For my son, Martin

—T.R.

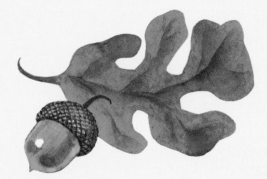

There is a legend
ravens tell, a
legend about a
wizard; a witch;
and a stout, tall tree.

The tree

grew high on a mountaintop, up where the thunder starts and the ravens soar. Tiny red flowers bloomed in the grass under the tree, and jays plucked acorns from its branches and buried them among its roots.

It was a perfect tree to climb, and Stefan and his little sister Gaila had claimed it for their own. Every day they came to play beneath it.

One day a wizard, walking across the mountaintops, stopped before the tree.

"Good day, sir," said Stefan. "Won't you come rest in the shade of our tree?"

"The moss is soft to sit on," offered Gaila.

The wizard sat down. He smiled and breathed deeply, and looked out across the valley. At last, he rose.

He patted the tree trunk and said, "What a good rest I've had under this fine tree. In thanks, I will make you a promise: One day this tree will be part of a beautiful castle, and it will bring great happiness."

Stefan and Gaila clapped their hands. A castle! How exciting!

But one dark and gusty day soon after, a witch came to the mountaintop. Her hair hung around her face like dead weeds in the fog. Trudging wearily along the mountain path, the witch stumbled on one of the tree's thick roots.

"Wretched tree!" she shrieked. "Curse on you!"

Stefan and Gaila ran up to her, waving their arms and crying.

"This is a wonderful tree," Stefan protested. "The wizard has promised that one day it will be part of a beautiful castle and bring great happiness."

"Well, well, well," said the witch in her icicle voice.

"I cannot undo the wizard's promise. But I can add a curse of my own." She shook a crooked finger at the children, then pointed to the tree. "Your tree may become part of a beautiful castle, *but* on the day it is finished, armies will attack and it will fall with a *crash!* And it will take more power than a wizard has to build your precious castle back!"

The witch's cackle echoed down the mountainside. Birds flew up from the trees in panic.

The children worried for days and days. Then, once again, the wizard came to the mountaintop. They told him the terrible tale. The wizard paced around and around the tree, trying to think of a way to outwit the witch.

"There is only one way," he said at last. "Your tree *will* be part of a beautiful castle, and it will bring great happiness. The witch has said that it will fall, and fall it will. And I cannot build it back. But do not fear. Hands not strong will build your castle and they will have the power to build it back."

The man of magic twirled around and around until the stars on his cape looked as if they were flying through the air. Suddenly he stopped and threw out his arms, pointing straight at the tree. From a cloudless sky a great clap of thunder rang out. A streak of jagged lightning flashed and struck the tree, leaving a deep, black scar along the length of its trunk.

"All will be well," the wizard declared, and he wrapped his cape around himself and went on his way.

The tree remained there on the mountaintop. Storms came, but the tree stood stout and tall. Baby birds called to their mothers from nests safely hidden. Butterflies made whisper-landings on the branches, and ravens rested at the very top.

Every day, Stefan and Gaila played under the tree. They trusted the wizard and believed his promise. But they did not understand his riddle about hands not strong, and they did not understand why he had called down lightning to strike their tree. And, of course, they feared the witch and her dreadful curse.

One day, men came in a wagon, cutting trees. Their hands looked big and strong as they lifted the trunk of Stefan and Gaila's tree onto the wagon.

"We will be building a grand new castle for the king," the men said.

Month after month, the builders worked and the castle took shape. Stefan and Gaila watched, wondering where the wood from their tree would be used. Perhaps it would form a strong doorway, or perhaps a smooth, gleaming floor for dancing.

The day the castle was finished, the king gave a party to celebrate. Happy throngs of people streamed into the magnificent castle. Stefan and Gaila went, too, looking high and low for signs of the wood from their tree. They passed through a strong wooden doorway, and they walked on a gleaming wooden floor, but they couldn't tell if the wood came from their tree.

And then, in a dark hallway, they saw the witch, walking slowly toward them. Her voice was even more terrifying than ever.

"You had better run for your lives, my little dears. Remember, before this day has ended, armies will attack and the castle will fall!"

Suddenly, shouts came from a chamber at the end of the corridor.

"The army is here! It is on the attack! Man the battlements!"

After the shouts came a sound the children dreaded—a crash. Not loud, though. What was happening?

Gaila and Stefan ran to the chamber. The witch chased after them, cackling with delight. They rushed to the nearest window. Outside they saw sunshine and rolling hills. A raven flew by and the spring breeze touched their cheeks. Where was the army?

The children turned around in confusion. And then they saw the little prince sitting on the floor. Around him stood armies of toy soldiers, and in the center lay a pile of wooden blocks.

"The blue army has destroyed the castle," announced the prince. "But it's all right. I'll fix it. You can help, too, if you want."

Smiling, he began to rebuild block walls and towers. "This will be a castle again soon."

Gaila picked up one of the blocks. The wood was beautiful indeed, but along one side ran a black scar. She handed the block to Stefan.

"I guess because the lightning marked the tree, the carpenters cut the wood into blocks for the prince," he said.

The children smiled at each other. At last they understood the wizard's plan.

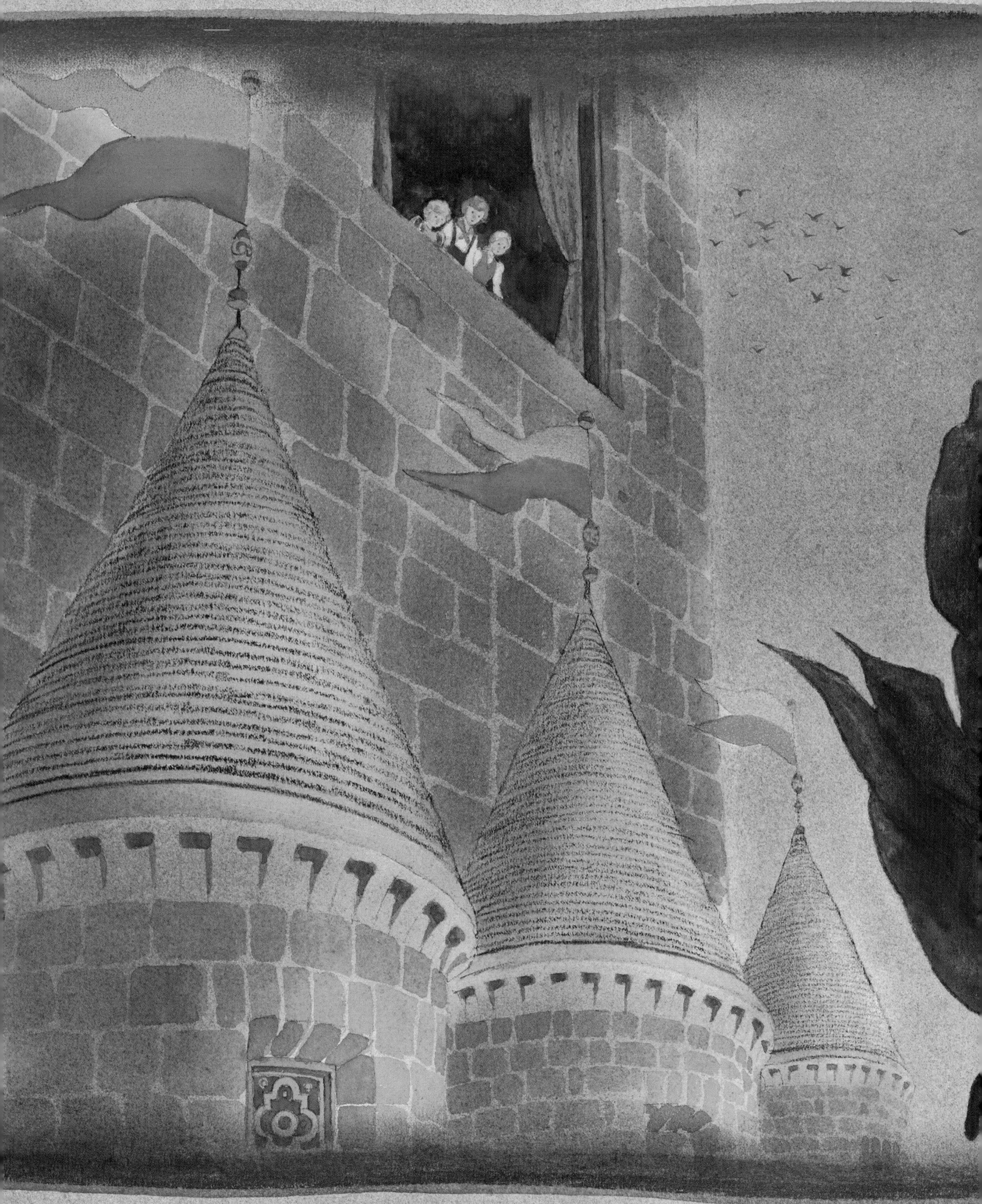

"Why are you smiling?" demanded the witch. "Your lives are in danger. I said the castle will fall and fall it will!"

"The castle *has* fallen," replied Gaila happily. "All castles of blocks fall and little hands build them back."

"But—but my curse...." stammered the witch.

"Your curse came true," said Stefan. "But it couldn't hurt the wizard's promise."

Too angry to speak, the witch picked up her black skirts and jumped out the window. She ran over the rolling hills, out of sight, and was never seen again.

Across the valley from the castle, a new tree stands now where the old one grew. It sprouted from an acorn a jay forgot to fetch.

Baby birds call to their mothers from nests hidden in its leaves. And the tree is easy to climb.

Ravens rest at the top and tell the story of the beautiful little castle inside the big castle, and of the happiness it brought.

Storms shake the tree, but it stands stout and tall, up where the thunder starts and the ravens soar.